# COLORING BOOK
# ABOUT THE
# ANGELS

Pictures and Rhymes by EMMA C. McKEAN

**WITH UNDERLINED WORDS IN RHYME**

## CATHOLIC BOOK PUBLISHING CORP.
New Jersey

Jesus wants all children
To grow in faith and <u>grace</u>,
Knowing that their Angels
See His FATHER'S <u>FACE</u>.

JESUS, LORD and SAVIOR,
We come to You and <u>pray</u>,
"Bless us as we lovingly
Follow in YOUR <u>WAY</u>."

(T-672)

© 1984 Catholic Book Publishing Corp., N.J.
Printed in China

NIHIL OBSTAT: Daniel V. Flynn, J.C.D., *Censor Librorum*
IMPRIMATUR: Joseph T. O'Keefe,
*Administrator, Archdiocese of New York*
www.catholicbookpublishing.com

JESUS
loves
little children.

I talk to my Guardian Angel,
A spirit friend, I do not <u>see</u>.
My Angel sees the Face of God,
And brings His Light to <u>me</u>.

I thank Our Father in heaven,
For the Angel helper, <u>Who</u>—
Is always very close to God,
And helps me—<u>to be, too</u>.

Jerry and Gina are thinking about
Two Old Testament Prophets and <u>may</u>
Learn from their Picture Bibles—
\more—
About <u>Jeremiah</u> and <u>Isaiah, today</u>.

JEREMIAH

ISAIAH

TOBIAH

When Tobiah, son of Tobit,
Traveled far <u>away</u>,
The Angel Raphael was his
  guide,
To help him on his <u>way</u>.

St. Raphael told Tobiah
What parts of a fish would <u>be</u>
Useful at home for his father
  here,
As a cure so his father could
  <u>see</u>.

Daniel, the Old Testament prophet,
Would go home, from work, to <u>pray</u>,
To kneel and give thanks to the LIVING GOD,
Three times every <u>day</u>.

Unjustly, for this reason,
He was put in the lions' <u>den</u>.
But God's Angel closed the lions' mouths,
So the lions did not harm him <u>then</u>.

DANIEL

11

The Angel Gabriel told Mary
when the HOLY SPIRIT
    came over her, that <u>SHE</u>
Became the Blessed Virgin
    MOTHER of JESUS.
The SON OF GOD IS <u>HE</u>.

MARY,
Mother of JESUS

13

# WHEN JESUS WAS BORN

Shepherds watching sheep,
Keeping them in <u>sight</u>,
Heard a shining Angel bring
Wondrous news to <u>light</u>,

About the newborn Savior,
Who in a manger <u>lay</u>,
In Bethlehem's city of David
Not very far <u>away</u>.

14

15

# WHERE JESUS WAS BORN

Many Angels appeared and
were singing,
The wonderful hymn of <u>joy</u>,
As the shepherds saw,
The Son of God,
The Infant Savior <u>Boy</u>.

Joseph dreamed an Angel
Told him to get up and <u>flee</u>,
With Baby Jesus and Mary to
　　Egypt,
At that time—a safe place to <u>be</u>.

To Egypt, the Holy Family
Quietly, that night went to <u>stay</u>.
But one day returned to Nazareth,
When the Angel told Joseph
　　they <u>may</u>.

In the Temple, when Jesus was twelve,
The elders were amazed to <u>hear</u>
Jesus tell about His FATHER IN HEAVEN,
As the LIGHT of the LORD shone <u>clear</u>.

# BEFORE JESUS DIED
## on the Cross at Calvary

While Jesus was sad in the Garden,
The three Apostles who were there,
    failed to <u>keep</u>
On waiting, and watching with Him;
Peter, James, and John, fell <u>asleep</u>.

Three times, He prayed.
Then an Angel,
Gave the strength He needed to <u>take</u>,
The heavy Cross to Calvary,
For the world's Salvation <u>sake</u>.

# WHEN JESUS ROSE FROM the DEAD

Some women went looking for Jesus;
In the tomb where His Body once <u>lay</u>,
Two Angels were waiting to greet them;
One had a message to <u>say</u>.

A glorious thing had happened.
Christ was risen—no longer was <u>dead</u>.
The women should tell His disciples,
Christ would see them in Galilee, he <u>said</u>.

24

# WHEN JESUS ASCENDED INTO HEAVEN

Forty days after Christ's Resurrection,
He blessed His disciples, who were to <u>see</u>,
His glorious Ascension to heaven,
From a mountain, in <u>Galilee</u>.

And then when they no longer could
see Him;
Shining Angels appeared to <u>explain</u>,
Though Jesus had risen to heaven,
He would come from heaven to earth,
once <u>again</u>!

The children of the choir, lovingly,
Join the Angels, in sweet <u>accord</u>,
As they sing the glorious hymn
of praise:

"HOLY, HOLY,

HOLY <u>LORD. . . .</u>"

These children saw a picture
of Saint Stanislaus and <u>know</u>
He received Holy Communion
from an Angel,
More than 400 years <u>ago</u>.

PICTURE
BOOK OF
SAINTS

To make shining lights, trace over all straight lines, with orange and yellow crayons.

Practice here

32